My First

Disney Classics

LIBRARY

The Soaring Star!

PaRragon

Bath · New York · Singapore · Hong Kong · Cologne · Delhi
Melbourne · Amsterdam · Johannesburg · Auckland · Shenzhen

This edition published by Parragon in 2010

Parragon
Queen Street House
4 Queen Street
Bath BA1 1HE, UK

Adapted by Mathew Ferguson
Illustrated by Disney Storybook Artists
Designed by Jerome Rebeiro

ISBN 978-1-4454-2409-5
Printed in China

The Soaring Star!

Mathew Ferguson

It was the first day of spring, and every mother animal in the circus had a new baby to love—every mother except for Mrs Jumbo, that is. Her baby elephant had not arrived.

The following day, the circus animals were all travelling in a train when they heard a strange voice.

'Oh, Mrs Jumbo!' the voice said. 'Special delivery for Mrs Jumbo!' It was Mr Stork!

Mr Stork flew down into the elephants' carriage, approached Mrs Jumbo, and dropped a bundle at her feet.

Mrs Jumbo's baby had arrived!

'It's little Jumbo!' said all of the elephants. They agreed that he was a beautiful baby.

But then the tiny elephant sneezed, and his ears flapped out. They were the biggest ears that any of the elephants had ever seen! Because of his enormous ears, the other elephants decided to call him Dumbo.

Mrs Jumbo didn't care what the other elephants said. She cradled Dumbo in her trunk and rocked him to sleep.

Dumbo soon joined the circus with his mother. But people always made fun of his ears! Children teased him, and adults laughed at him.

One day, some children pulled his ears!

Mrs Jumbo didn't like seeing her baby treated badly, so she reared up and scared the children away.

The circus owners saw her and thought she was dangerous. They locked her in a cage!

Dumbo was left all alone. The other elephants said that he was a disgrace to elephants everywhere because of his big ears. But Timothy Q. Mouse believed that Dumbo would be a star one day!

Timothy thought up a great plan—Dumbo could perform in a circus act!

That night, the mouse crept into the Ringmaster's caravan and whispered the idea to the sleeping man. The very next day, Dumbo's act was added as a highlight to the show!

That night, Dumbo got ready to perform. As he waited by the sidelines, the other elephants climbed on top of each other and created a giant elephant pyramid. Then it was up to Dumbo to leap to the top of the pyramid.

Dumbo ran onto the springboard and jumped ...

... but he tripped over his ears and collided with the pyramid of elephants! The elephants swayed back and forth, and then fell to the ground. They broke the pole at the centre of the circus tent!

Soon, the entire tent collapsed. What a disaster! Dumbo's starring role was immediately cancelled, and he was demoted to being a clown.

In his clown act, Dumbo had to jump out of a high window while firemen put out a fake fire. Everyone in the crowd laughed at Dumbo's big ears.

Dumbo was miserable. His mother was still locked away, and he was the laughing-stock of the entire circus.

'Don't worry, Dumbo,' whispered Timothy. 'You'll be flying high one day!'

That night, Dumbo dreamed that he was the star of a magical circus. In the dream, elephants paraded around and danced. And at the end of the dream, Dumbo bounced off a springboard, high into the air—and away he flew!

The next morning, Timothy awoke to find five crows staring at him! 'What are you doing here?' asked the crows.

Timothy quickly realised that he and Dumbo were in a tree!

'You flew up here!' the crows said.

When Dumbo woke up, he fell out of the tree.
'You can fly!' Timothy shouted.
But try as he might, Dumbo just couldn't fly again.

The crows felt sorry for Dumbo. So one of them handed Dumbo a single black feather. 'Try this magic feather,' the crow said. 'Hold onto it, and you'll be able to fly!'

Dumbo held the magic feather in his trunk and prepared to jump from a cliff.

As he jumped, Dumbo didn't fall—he flew! Just like a bird, he soared over the tallest treetops. He glided and dipped and dived with the crows.

'We'll keep your flying a secret until this afternoon's show,' said Timothy.

That afternoon, Dumbo was ready to perform in his clown act. He stood at the top of a tall, burning building, ready to jump onto a mat below. But this time, he would fly! 'Good luck, Dumbo!' Timothy cheered.

Dumbo leaped from the tower, but he dropped the magic feather! He started to fall like a stone.

'The feather was a trick!' Timothy shouted as they fell. 'You can fly by yourself!'

Dumbo didn't believe it, but he spread his ears wide ...

... and he flew! Dumbo swooped into the air, over the amazed crowd. They leaped to their feet and cheered as Dumbo did loops, spins, and rolls. It was simply incredible!

Because of Dumbo's incredible display, people started flocking to the circus. The act became a huge hit, and Dumbo became famous. He was even in the newspapers!

But best of all, Dumbo got to see his mother again. From then on, Dumbo, Timothy, and Mrs Jumbo travelled all over the country as the stars of Dumbo's Flying Circus.

The End.